給保羅的禮物

A Present
For Paul

MANTRA

Text copyright © Bernard Ashley 1996
Illustrations copyright © David Mitchell 1996
Dual language text copyright © Mantra Publishing Ltd 1997
The author/illustrator asserts the moral right to be
identified as the author/illustrator of this Work.

Published by arrangement with HarperCollins Publishers Ltd in 1996
All Rights Reserved

Printed in Hong Kong by South China Printing Co (1988) Ltd

Published by
Mantra Publishing Ltd
5 Alexandra Grove
London N12 8NU
http://www.mantrapublishing.com

給保羅的禮物

A Present
For Paul

BERNARD ASHLEY   **DAVID MITCHELL**

Chinese Translation by Sylvia Denham

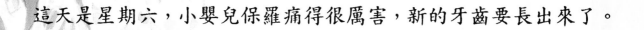

這天是星期六，小嬰兒保羅痛得很屬害，新的牙齒要長出來了。

It was Saturday and baby Paul was hurting badly with a new tooth coming through.

歡樂的爸爸説他會去市場購物，並會帶他的大女孩一起去。
「但你必須緊緊貼著我，」他對她説，「今天市場會很擠擁。」

Pleasure's dad said he'd do the shopping at the market and
take his big girl. "But you'd better stay close," he told her. "The
market is a busy place today."

從巴士上層望去，市場好像展覽會一般有趣。
「我有一鎊，我會買一份禮物給保羅，」歡樂說。
但爸爸正忙著看他的購物目錄單。

From the top of the bus the market looked good fun like a fair.
"I have a pound for a present for Paul," Pleasure said.
But her dad was busy checking his list.

市場喧鬧嘈吵，而爸爸又有那麼多的東西要買。他緊緊抓著
歡樂，買了辣椒、馬鈴薯和扁豆。歡樂望著玩具，希望能夠買
到東西給保羅。

It was all bustle and bags at the market. And Dad with all that
shopping to do. Holding her tightly he bought chillies, potatoes and
beans. Pleasure was eyeing the toys, wanting to get something for Paul.

「鮮魚，」爸爸説著，讓歡樂選擇，但她沒有認眞看。保羅不會要鱈魚的，他會喜歡一個會響的玩具。

"Fresh fish," Dad said, letting Pleasure choose. But she didn't give it too much of a look. Paul wouldn't want haddock, but he'd like a rattle.

當爸爸放手付錢時，歡樂把手直放進袋去，因為那邊有一個
出牙用的橡皮環－剛好適合嬰兒咬。

When Dad let go to pay, her hand went straight into her pocket.
Because over there was a teething ring - just right for the baby to bite.

她轉身笑著對爸爸說，正想著保羅會多麼高興─但她的笑容瞬間消失。
「爸爸…！」

She twisted round smiling to tell Dad. She was thinking how pleased Paul would be - but the smile was wiped off in a flash.
"Dad...!"

她的爸爸走了！他不在那裡？他究竟在那兒？他怎能走得這麼快？她到處張望—但她只能見到陌生人的腿和他們的外衣及袋。

Her dad had gone! *He wasn't there?* Where was he? How could he have gone so quick? She looked - but all she could see were strangers' legs and their coats and their bags.

人人都在那裡，就是沒有他的蹤影！她的心緒零亂—爸爸常
說她是他的大女孩，所以她是不會驚慌的！

There was everyone else, but no sign of him! Her stomach
did a head over heels - he always said she was his big girl, so
she wasn't going to get scared!

她在腿叢中穿插，她站在腳尖上，爸爸不會在遠處的。

She pushed through legs, she stood on her toes. He couldn't be far.

她向舊貨攤處望，他就在那裡！她果然是對的。

She looked at the second hand stall. There he was! She was right.

她在人叢中穿插...

She ran through the crowd...

...並抓緊他的運動裝。

... and grabbed hard at his tracksuit.

但運動裝的條子不同，連面孔也不一樣。

But the striping was different and so was the face.

現在歡樂真的驚慌了，好像世界上只有她一個小孩。

Now Pleasure *did* feel frightened, like the only child in the world.

「她迷失了！」有人說道，「可憐的小孩！」

"She's lost!" someone said. "The poor little mite!"

整團人盯著她，圍著她，

A whole staring ring of them crowding her in,

好像圍捕一隻受了傷的小鳥。

like trapping a wounded bird.

她轉身便跑，不知道往那裡去，總之是遠離他們的手和叫喊聲。

他必定在某處地方！

She turned and ran, she
didn't know where, but
away from their hands
and their shouts. He'd got
to be somewhere!

她大聲叫：「爸爸！」並在貨攤間追跑...

She shouted, "DAD!" and chased through the stalls...

在衣裙、水果、鮮花及手袋之間穿插。

...through dresses and fruit and flowers and bags.

直至她慌張地跑叫到最後一個貨攤，那個魚...一他正在那裡數他的零錢。「究竟甚麼事，小女孩？」

他根本沒有留意惦記著她。

Till she came shouting in panic round one last stall, to the fish - where he was counting his change.
"What's the matter with you, girl?"
He hadn't missed her at all.

她緊緊抓著他
以防再次失去他。

She grabbed him
in case she lost him
again.

「你剛才在那裡？」她哭著說。
「我在那兒？我沒有移動過一寸。」

"Where were you?" she cried.
"Where was I? I haven't budged an inch."

他跟著輕聲地安撫她說：「你迷失前有沒有找到禮物給保羅？」

He then spoke softly to calm her down. "Did you choose a present for Paul before you lost sight of me?"

歡樂點頭，她從眼淚中看到它。
「那個...出牙用的...橡皮環，」她對他說。

Pleasure nodded her head and through her tears she saw it.
"The...teething...ring," she told him.

「那個很好。驚慌過後要不要一些安慰的東西？」他說著，
心裡想送她一樣好東西。

"That's nice. And what about something for a bit of comfort after
a scare?" he said wanting to give her a treat.

歡樂再看看那個貨攤，心裡沒有他那大女孩的感覺。
「我想要一個洋娃娃，」她說道，「但我最好還是要那個
嬰兒橡皮環！」

Pleasure looked at the stall again, not feeling like his big girl.
"I'd like a doll," she said, "but I'd better have that babies' dummy!"

爸爸的笑容令甚麼都沒事了。

And his smile made everything right.